Investi GATORS
Heist and Seek

written and illustrated by
John Patrick Green

with colour by **Wes Dzioba**

MACMILLAN CHILDREN'S BOOKS

For Klaus, and art teachers everywhere

First published 2022 by First Second

This edition published in the UK 2022 by Macmillan Children's Books
an imprint of Pan Macmillan
The Smithson, 6 Briset Street, London EC1M 5NR
EU representative: Macmillan Publishers Ireland Ltd, 1st Floor,
The Liffey Trust Centre, 117-126 Sheriff Street Upper
Dublin 1, D01 YC43
Associated companies throughout the world
www.panmacmillan.com

ISBN 978-1-5290-9719-1

1 3 5 7 9 8 6 4 2

A CIP catalogue record for this book is available from the British Library.

Cover design by John Patrick Green and Kirk Benshoff
Interior book design by John Patrick Green
Colour by Wes Dzioba

Printed in China

Other books by John Patrick Green

InvestiGators

InvestiGators: Take the Plunge

InvestiGators: Off the Hook

InvestiGators: Ants in Our P.A.N.T.S.

InvestiGators: Braver and Boulder

Chapter 1

It's an exciting day, as precious cargo enters the country...

Hurry up loading that art!

...and makes its way towards the city!

DETECTIVE COLE!

With the city's **best detective** my hostage, the mayor has no choice but to pay my ransom, or I'll turn this town into *dust!*

Well, not *dust.* Sugar. Because I like to eat sugar.

You may be a **weevil**...but you don't have to be **EVIL!** Listen to me—

To *YOU?* The only leafy green I listen to is *COLD, HARD CASH!*

NO ONE CAN STOP ME! Not even the—

*Very Exciting Spy Technology

6

Agents! You're urgently needed at the city **Art Museum!**

The art museum? What is it?

It's a big building where people can look at art.

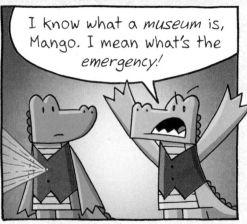

I know what a *museum* is, Mango. I mean what's the *emergency!*

An armoured car was transporting priceless works of art to the museum for an upcoming exhibit. But when it arrived, the paintings were nowhere to be seen!

Oh, no!

And art is MEANT to be seen!

Among these historical works was the **"Bona Lisa"**, by Leodoggo da Vinky!
Da Vinky?
Mango, Brash. Your **mission** is to *track down* those missing paintings and *catch* whoever's responsible!
Good luck, agents!
We'll get right on it, General Inspector...
Vrp
Beep

Chapter 2

Dang, it's closed. Guess we'll just have to go see a movie instead.

Let's find the staff entrance.

Agents of S.U.I.T.*? Sounds fancy-pants.

I'm Savanna, the museum preparator. I prepare the art for the exhibits.

Ow.

Who was in the armoured car when the art disappeared?

That'd be T and P.

T and P...? As in toilet paper?

OH! T and P, as in Tortoise and Porpoise!

Tell us what happened, T and P.

Nothin' unusual at first!

*Special Undercover Investigation Teams

13

14

But when we opened 'er up, the van was **completely empty!**

Beep

vrrt

Hmm... This clearly wasn't the work of a mere cat burglar.

Meerkat?

Can't explain it any better than we could the last time this happened.

How long ago was that?

Yesterday!

Almost EVERY piece of art for the gala vanished outta this van on its way to the museum.

Gala?

The big red-carpet shindig later this week.

Is any *more* art expected to arrive for this gala?

My boss, the **museum curator,** would know. You can find him inside.

Thanks, Savanna.

Chapter 3

For all the art to *vanish* like that, this must've been—

A **MAGICIAN!**

No, wait...

A **GHOST!** The armoured car is *HAUNTED!* It was a *POLTERHEIST!*

What? NO, Mango. I was going to say "an inside job".

Pfft, **inside job.** Why can't it be an **OUTSIDE job** for once? The weather's so nice!

But they're **ALL GONE!**

The only artwork for the gala that *HAS* arrived is a piece by **Panksy!**

Panksy? The former possum street artist? I mean, possum former street artist?

Didn't he have a YooToob channel where he pulled pranks on people?

Yeah, he had a catchphrase and everything!

AAAH!

You got Panksy'd!

3,263,827 views

24

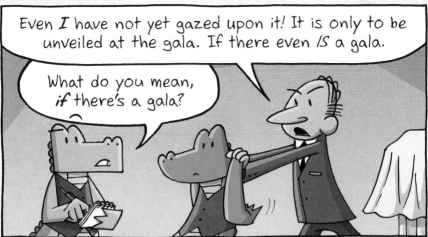

Panksy's piece alone isn't enough for a whole gala. Unless some **artistic genius** emerges from obscurity with a masterpiece I can display alongside Panksy's, the event can't go on!

And then the museum will be closed...*permanently!* Without the gala, the city council will have just the excuse they need to **defund the arts!**

De-fun the arts? Why? Art is *SO MUCH* fun!

Indeed. But there'll be no more school trips... No more smiling faces of the children laughing at the Bootycellis... And, most tragically, no more fancy galas!

*See **InvestiGators** books 1–5!

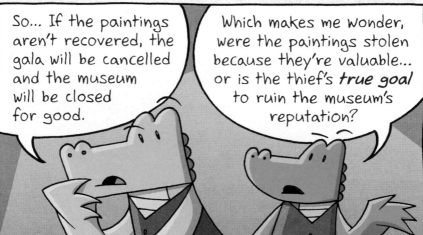

MANGO! I have an idea how to *flush out* whoever's responsible for the missing paintings.

We need to get to **S.U.I.T. Headquarters!**

Well, speaking of *flush,* we can flush *ourselves* into the sewer to get there!

I'll be right behind you!

plonk!

floosh!

Down the hatch!

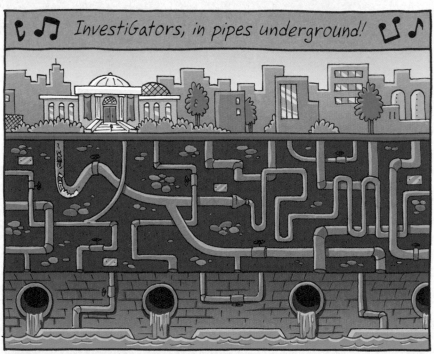

Below the city, in S.U.I.T.'s secret headquarters...

Chapter 4

What we need to do, Mango, is set a **TRAP** for whoever tries to steal the *NEXT* piece of art that's heading to the museum for the gala.

But, Brash, the curator said there *isn't* any more art on the way. *UNLESS...*

...**WE** become artistic geniuses whose artwork can be added to the exhibit!

EXACTAMUNDO! We create a masterpiece or two, *easy peasy*, get invited to display them at the gala and then **catch** the thief when they try to steal our art as it's being transported in the armoured car.

Sounds simple enough!

*Computerized Ocular Remote Butler

38

43

Hello, Susan? Have I found a TALENT for you! No, no, not another **CARTOONIST** – a *REAL* artist!

Chapter 5

Sven is taking longer than usual. Your disguise must be some Very **COMPLICATED** Spy Technology!

V.C.S.T.? Doesn't exactly roll off the tongue.

Ah, Sven!

Sorry for the wait, Gators. Due to the unique requirements for Mango's disguise, instead of a V.E.S.T., I've come up with...

...a **S.M.O.C.K.!**

It stands for:

Supplementing **M**ango's **O**riginality, **C**reativity and **K**nowledge!

Supplementing?

Yeah, it means "extra".

It doesn't *LOOK* extra.

Try it on, Mango.

What's this button do?

Borp

...and *THAT'S* why you don't look a gift horse in the mouth. Now for the **Arts and Vulture** report—

MMPH!

NEIGHbours, amirite?

SORRY! The **Arts and** *CULTURE* report!

Over to you, Vohnda.

No worries, Cici. Happens *ALL* the time.

A previously unknown artistic genius has just emerged in the art world. *SO* unknown that I didn't even ask his name before booking this **exclusive remote interview!**

LIVE from somewhere

Greetings, Vohnda. My name is MA—

≥PST!≤

Tap Tap

YOU'RE UNDERCOVER

—AAAAAcaroni...

Macaroni what?

LIVE from somewhe

Macaroniiiiii...aaaaaan' cheese?

I'm not familiar with **Lamparugalightswitchland**. Is it a small country?

Oh, it's tiny. Like the size of this room.

Can you tell us a bit about what inspired your latest painting?

This piece was inspired by... fruit...that grows here in... Lamparugalightswitchland.

I call it... "Rhapsody in Fruit".

It is *MAHVELLOUS*. I can almost *TASTE* the colours!

LIVE from Lamparugalightswitchland

53

Chapter 6

Gators! Susan says the curator wants Macaroni's "Rhapsody in Fruit" in the museum exhibit!

Just in time! The gala's tomorrow night!

The armoured car will be at the airport first thing in the morning to pick up your art once you "arrive" from Lamparugalightswitchland after a lay-over in Frankfurt.

Air quotes

I do like frankfurters, but you couldn't get me a direct flight?

Mango, you're not actually flying anywhere. Lamparugalightswitchland doesn't exist!

Oh, right.

Now, let's see...

OPERATION ART TRAP
1) Become artistic geniuses ✓
2) Get invited to gala ✓
3) Catch burglar

57

58

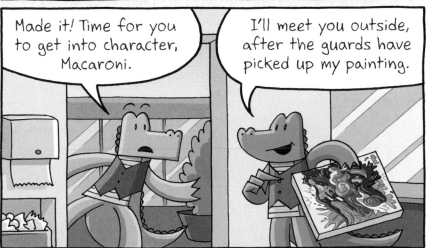

Woulda been polite of them to offer me a *ride*, at least!

Over here, Mangoroni! I mean — Macaroni!

The trap is set, Brash. Now to see who falls for it!

Let me just turn off these **art layers**...

Borp

Zep zop zip

...and get back into **InvestiGator mode**!

Chapter 7

The armoured car is about a block away.

It's still heading toward the museum. Is your canvas still in the back?

As far as I can tell.

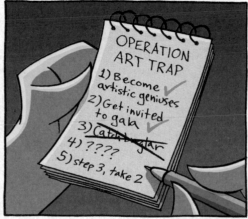

Chapter 8

At the CORRECT museum...

&3 ART MUSEUM &3

When T and P returned with *yet another* empty armoured car, I feared the worst. But you've found *all* the missing paintings, just in time for the gala! I won't have to cancel it after all!

We would've been here sooner, but we went to the **UDDER** museum.

We **HERD** they had an impressive **CATTLE**-log. It was quite **MOO**-ving.

But we made sure to **HOOF** it over before it was **PASTURE** bedtime.

Don't **MILK** the joke, Mango.

Thank you for recovering the art, InvestiGators. *Especially* the Macaroni Ancheese piece.

It would've been **most embarrassing** if I had to tell Macaroni I lost his painting *to his face!*

Don't worry, my lips are sealed.

Zip

Vincent van Gopher's "The Starry Night".

Seeing this in person for the first time, I never noticed the **texture** before.

You're very observant.

Hardly anyone *REALLY* looks at art that closely. They'll glance at it for two seconds and move on.

Well, I'm sure everyone at the gala will be excited to see all these masterpieces.

FEH! This gala is just an excuse for people to *hobnob* and *take selfies* with **famous celebrities.**

Sadly, all the best artists were not *appreciated* in their lifetimes.

Modern artists don't have any *discipline*. They'd rather make art into a *joke*.

Like that Panksy.

More like **PRANK**sy! His idea of art is replacing the water in the park fountain with *prune juice!*

You got Panksy'd!

I told you you'd get your money AFTER the job was completed.

Well, that was YESTERDAY. Things have CHANGED since then.

If I don't pull this off TONIGHT, then neither of us gets *ANYTHING!*

You're still in? Good!

What, *really?* Oh. Well, fine. No one will know, trust me. It will be our little secret.

Something tells me that *little secret* will be a *BIG DEAL!*

Now, **Macaroni Ancheese** is a *TRUE* artist. He's clearly studied and respects the works by the masters. I look forward to meeting him at the gala.

Well, as it turns out—

⋛PSST!⋚ Mango!

What is it, Brash?

Not here. C'mon, I'll tell you outside.

Don't you find it awfully *suspicious* that the curator doesn't want InvestiGators at the gala with the art thief still on the loose?

&3 ART MUSEUM &3

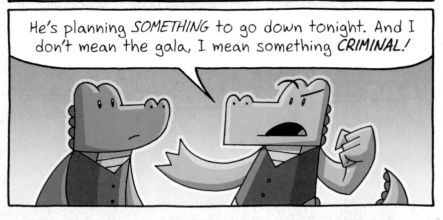

He's planning *SOMETHING* to go down tonight. And I don't mean the gala, I mean something *CRIMINAL!*

Do you have any **proof?**

Not yet. That's why we need to go *undercover* at the gala so we can catch him in the act!

Ooh! I can go in disguise as Macaroni Ancheese. But there isn't enough time before the gala for you to get a new V.E.S.T. from Sven. How will you get in?

You'll just have to WAIT and see.

scritch scratch

Is this about the weight of the paintings again?

No, WAIT as in – *AH,* forget it.

Chapter 9

This is Cici Boringstories with *Action News Now*, reporting LIVE from outside the city **Art Museum Gala**! I'm filling in for Vohnda, the Culture Vulture, who's out sick with **avian flu.**

I don't care much for *boring old art*, but I'll never pass up an opportunity for **celebrity gawking.** Catching a glimpse of a famous face is quite a competition amongst the **paparazzi!**

Enough *clowning* around, Cici. More guests are here!

Actors! Musicians! Athletes! All *dressed* to *impress!*

And even **Dr. Doodledoo** from the **Science Factory!**

He's not *CHICKEN* to make a bold fashion statement.

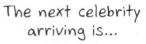

Wow, look at all the people. And the *detail!* Now that I'm an artist, I can appreciate just how much work goes into drawing a page like this.

I hope the scene of Brash sneaking into the gala is easier to draw.

Chapter 10

shuff

This should do the trick.

Really? No one's said anything?

Everyone thinks they're great so far.

Okay, then. Have the waiters keep bringing them out.

Mango, I'm in.

Mango?

beep

Ooh, *hors d'oeuvres!*

Mmm, shrimp and garlic!

Ancheese!

And cheese? I don't taste cheese...

Oh, that's *ME!*

Mr. Ancheese. I'm Savanna, the museum preparator. What do you think of the exhibit?

Oh, well I—

V R B T

You're...shivering. Are you cold?

Uh, YES!

The weather is much warmer in Lamparugalightswitchland. That's why I'm wearing this scarf and am, *uh*...blue.

VRBT!

Mango? Why won't he answer?

Beep Beep

What do you think you're doing?

Get out there and serve those hors d'oeuvres! They won't stay fresh forever.

And remember, they're for the *GUESTS* only!

Er, yes, boss!

NOW I get it. "WAIT and see". You're a WAITER! An **InvestiWAITER.**

You sure made me WAIT a long time for *THAT* set-up to pay off!

Remember, **MACARONI,** we're not here for hobnobbing and finger food. Keep your eyes peeled for anything or any*ONE* suspicious.

May I have everyone's attention? I am the museum curator, Thelonious Snoot.

It is time to unveil the *pièce de résistance!*

Oooh!

Aah!

Magnificent!

It's...a brick?

It's a commentary on the foundation of society!

It distills brutalism to the simplest expression!

≥Sigh≤ I'm going to snoop around the curator's office.

Snoop on **Snoot**. Good idea. And maybe bring back more of those *shrimp things* when you have a chance.

Chapter 11

Here, see?

My niece made it for me!

That's not *REAL* art!

Savanna sure is passionate about these paintings.

munch munch

But who here could be passionate enough to *steal* them?

Art isn't about the CREATION. Art is about the REACTION.

I didn't **create** that brick. I found it in the road. But by putting it on a pedestal and *calling* it art, I made people **REACT.**

Take this **"Bona Lisa".** Sure, it was made with skill and talent. But what does it *SAY?*

Um... Bark? Woof? Bow wow?

Exactly! *BOW DOWN* to the art snobs who decide what's "good enough" to belong in a museum.

How many of those have you served?

Uh...all of them?

There's gotta be a clue in here somewhere.

These are all unpaid bills. This museum is *DROWNING* in debt!

There's no way this **fundraiser** could be enough to pay all these off.

What's this?

According to this, the museum would've got *MILLIONS* if we hadn't recovered the stolen art!

Mango's in danger. I've got to warn him!

C'mon, Macaroni... Answer this time!

Are you feeling okay? You're lookin' a little *green.*

Oh, th-that's normal. Just... ⟨URP⟩...d-don't jostle me.

VRBT

HUPBT

Hi, I'm **Dr. Jake Hardbones, brain surgeon.** You may also know me as **Doctor Copter,** the *Action News Now* helicopter in the sky.

As a brain surgeon, I know a lot about **stomachs.** Because some people *THINK* with their stomachs. And on the next few pages, everyone will be *TALKING* with their stomachs...if you catch my meaning.

What you are about to see is very graphic. This is a *graphic novel,* after all. If you'd like to avoid the unpleasantness, skip ahead to page, *oh,* let's say 121.

Otherwise, *HOLD ON TO YOUR POTATOES!*

Chapter 12

Let's see what's on the news, eh, Lock?

click

A WAVE OF VOMIT!

Nope, I'm out. Time for your walk!

This is Cici Boringstories with *Action Spews Now* — I mean, *NEWS Now!* Guests of tonight's gala are pouring out of the museum, along with **PUKE** pouring out of their mouths!

MUSEUM

The **curator** and **caterer** are in **cahoots!** He had the art insured for MILLIONS in case of theft, but since we foiled *that* plan she decided to sabotage the gala by *POISONING THE HORS D'OEUVRES!*

Yeah, I found that out the hard way. But I think it's mostly out of my system.

The museum's reputation is certainly ruined *now.* But what do they have to gain by it?

&3 ART MUSEUM &3

Everyone's outside revealing their innermost secrets. And by *innermost secrets* I mean the **contents of their stomachs!**

If everyone's outside...

128

...then that means the art is COMPLETELY UNGUARDED! What if this was just a *distraction* so it can be stolen again?

We've got to get back inside, *quick!* We can take a short cut by flushing ourselves into the sewer!

Do you mind if we cut?

Porta-potties aren't connected to the sewer, Mango!

Oh, right.

We'll just have to push through the crowd. Hurry!

Okay, just not *TOO* fast.

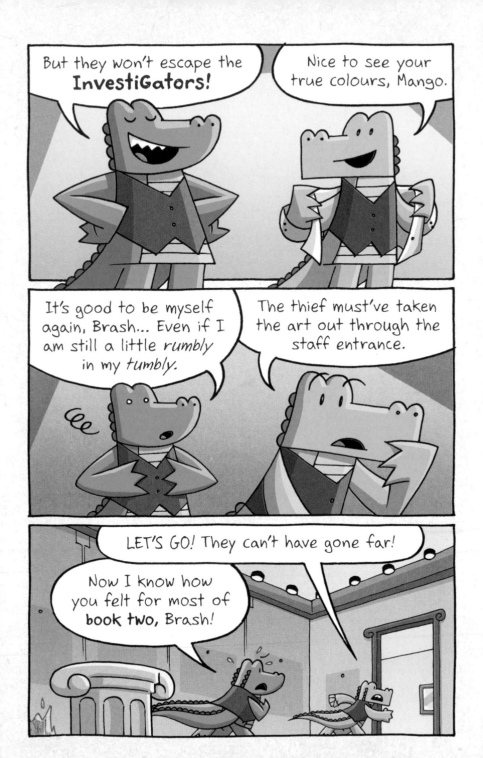

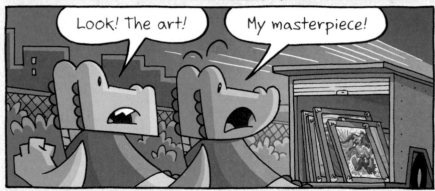

Look! The art!

My masterpiece!

They're getting away!

Chapter 13

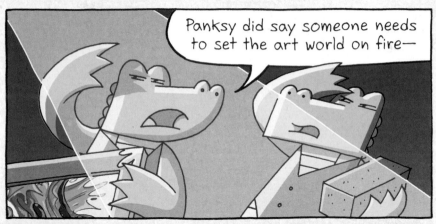

Chapter 14

You really messed up this time, InvestiGators. This is a **TAPESTRY!**

Wait... Tapestries are those **fancy fabrics** you hang on walls...

I mean **TRAVESTY!** You two let all the art from the gala go *UP IN SMOKE!*

SLAM

147

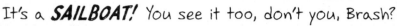

149

bip bip

Bip Bip Bip

Beep Beep Beep

We find it the same way we did last time, Brash. By following this tracker to my REAL painting!

Of course!

BEEP BEEP BEEP

Chapter 15

The thief can't have gone far. It hasn't been that long since the gala.

bip bip bip bip bip

THIS IS IT! My painting is somewhere above us!

Beep Beep

PAINT CHIP TRAKR

There's something familiar about this place...

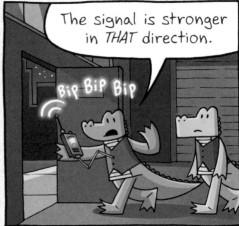

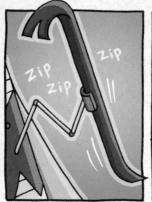

The missing masterpieces! And also your painting!

Let's make sure it really *is* mine...

Yup!

Whoever the forger is, they're *good*, but they missed my **signature**.

Brash! The tracker *WASN'T* out of alignment when we first found my painting. Because *THAT* wasn't *MY* painting. The tracker was pointing to my painting in *THIS* building the whole time!

So if the **REAL** art has been in here all along...then the paintings we returned to the museum were the **fakes?**

≋GASP!≋

The thief *WANTED* their forgeries to be found!

They painted their copies *here,* then moved them next door.

This *TOO OBVIOUS* hiding spot *WAS* meant to trick whoever showed up into searching the other building.

The copies of the original paintings were made to pull off a **switcheroo**, so the forgeries would get put on display at the gala. Our suspect must be—

A **KANGAROO!**

What? Where do you get "kangaroo"?

Well, you said "switcheroo", and that made me think of a kangaroo.

Not a kangaroo, Mango.

Our suspect must be someone with the right **MMO.**

Massive Multiplayer Online game?

Seriously, Mango? This is basic detective stuff! **MMO** stands for **M**eans, **M**otive and **O**pportunity.

I knew that. I just wanted to see if *YOU* knew that.

Panksy's an artist. And a prankster. He probably has the *MEANS* to create forgeries.

The **curator** insured the art for millions. Money makes for a pretty tempting *MOTIVE.*

And the **caterer** gave everyone food poisoning, which created the *OPPORTUNITY* to steal back the forgeries.

Well, we *KNOW* we have a lot of theories, but we don't have any **proof.**

Proof...?

THAT'S IT, Mango! The forgeries are **PROOF** of the crime!

If someone at the gala realized the paintings were *copies*, the hunt for the *originals* would be back on again.

They stole back the fakes to get rid of the **evidence!**

By destroying the forgeries in a fire, the whole world would believe the real art was lost forever in a botched burglary.

Exactamundo.

But they didn't factor in us saving the **fake** Macaroni. Shame the forger didn't sign it with their *OWN* name.

Shame they're not **here**. Then we'd know *FOR SURE* who did it.

We could wait around and see who shows up?

I've **WAITERED** enough for one evening! And they may not come back here until they know for certain they got away with the *perfect crime.*

What if...we can make the thief *THINK* they got away with it?

BRASH! I've got an **AMAZING** idea...

Chapter 16

I am Brash, an **InvestiGator** for S.U.I.T.! You're probably wondering why I invited you all here.

Invited? I work here! I've been here since last night!

Someone stole my catering truck and no one's offered me a ride home!

And I've got nowhere better to be!

You're here because each of you are **SUSPECTS** in last night's **disastrous art heist!**

If *I* did it, I wouldn't hang around the scene of the crime!

Yeah, I'd have skipped town!

EXACTLY! Fleeing would make you look *MORE* guilty. So you stayed to make me think you *DIDN'T* do it!

Preposterous!

Absurd!

Go on.

CURATOR SNOOT! YOU committed the crime so you'd get **MILLIONS** in insurance money to pay off the museum's debts!

What? NO! I mean, *yes*, the museum will get the insurance...

But I had nothing to make them with except **expired ingredients!** Because *SOMEONE* still hasn't paid me for *LAST YEAR'S* gala!

So it's PAYBACK you're after!

Don't look at *me*. Blame the city council!

And **PANKSY!** You don't buy into this *artsy-fartsy* nonsense. You stole the paintings as a **prank** to teach these snobs a lesson!

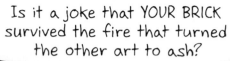

I'll admit, I do like a good joke.

Is it a joke that YOUR BRICK survived the fire that turned the other art to ash?

Panksy

I'm all for setting the art world on fire, but not *literally!* I was framed!

The *other* art was framed. *YOURS* was on a **PEDESTAL!**

It's *ALSO* suspicious that you're the only guest who didn't **THROW UP** from eating the hors d'oeuvres.

I'm a possum! I could eat trash all day and not get sick!

HMPH! Convenient.

Yes, it seems you three have PERFECT ALIBIS. Which is how I know the *REAL* thief is none other than...

...MACARONI ANCHEESE!

Buh-WHAAAA???

I was wondering when he'd get to you.

Macaroni stole the paintings the *FIRST* time just so that he'd get invited to have his work displayed at the gala!

Nuh-uh!

That's right! Macaroni was a **last-minute fill-in artist!**

I wasn't even in the country then! I was in Rugalampalightswitchland. *I MEAN,* Lamparuga-youknowtherest!

I bet that's not even a real place!

Macaroni was the first one to *throw up*. He got sick on *purpose!*

Er...

Did somebody say "porpoise"?

You didn't want to share the spotlight, so you **BARFED** all over the "Bona Lisa" so everyone would leave the museum.

I couldn't help it! I overate!

Like many artists, I don't know how to socialize at gatherings. I eat the whole time to avoid conversation!

Macaroni was also seen running *BACK* into the museum shortly after it was evacuated!

Well, that *IS* true...

169

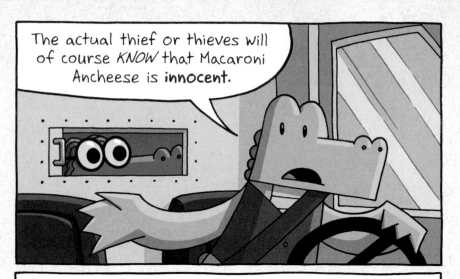

The actual thief or thieves will of course *KNOW* that Macaroni Ancheese is **innocent**.

But hopefully we've convinced them that *I* believe Macaroni did it. And now that Macaroni is going straight to jail, the **real criminal** is sure to think it's safe for them to go back to the storage unit.

And we'll be there to catch them *RED-HANDED!*

Or *whatever* colour paint may be on them from making *forgeries.*

ART MUSEUM

Chapter 17

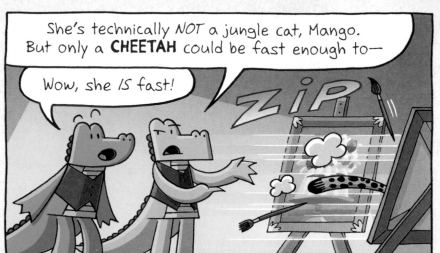

175

I've loved art ever since I was a little kid. I'd spend my time admiring it, studying it and copying other people's illustrations that I liked.

 There's nothing wrong with that. It's how *lots* of artists first learn how to draw.

 I went to art school, and as other students found their artistic voices, what I was best at was quickly mimicking everyone else's styles.

HEY! You *copycat!*

Imitation is the sincerest form of flattery, but the school still kicked me out!

Eventually, I got a job at the museum.

I've spent *years* looking at paintings. I mean, *REALLY* looking. Every **detail**, every **brushstroke**. No one appreciated them as much as I did!

So when the **most famous paintings in history** were coming to the museum for the gala, I was certain that if I painted copies and swapped them with the originals, no one would even notice.

I could keep the originals all to myself, and after the gala, **MY** art would be returned to museums all over the world for people to casually glance at.

Except you realized your forgeries *WEREN'T* perfect. So *YOU* poisoned the hors d'oeuvres because you were afraid someone was going to catch a mistake.

No! HONEST!

I *WANTED* people to *LOOK* at my art. Not **THROW UP** on it. When everyone got sick, my plan was *ruined!* My forgery skills can hold up to scrutiny, but the paint can't hold up to **STOMACH ACID.**

So that's when you decided to **evacuate** the museum, **destroy** the evidence and **frame** Panksy!

That was an accident! *Mostly...*

With the museum emptied, I thought I could sneak out my copies and repaint them. On the way out, I saw Panksy's *ridiculous brick.*

THIS isn't art! It doesn't *belong* in a museum!

Before I had a chance to lock the back of the armoured car, the brick *fell onto the gas pedal!*

WHOOPS!

DONK

VRRR

VROOM!

I stumbled back into the bushes as the van sped off without me!

PLOP!

I never intended to DESTROY my paintings. But if everyone *believed* the real ones were lost in a fire, at least I could still keep them all to myself.

I knew it would eventually come out that Macaroni Ancheese was **innocent**. But I figured I had time to paint *new* forgeries and hatch *another* plan to pass them off as the genuine articles.

Your phonies won't fool anyone now!

But I proved my point!

If I can paint just like the *best artists* in the world, then that makes **ME** the *best artist* in the world!

That's why I stole that Macaroni painting. I made an **EXACT COPY,** showed it to his **face** at the gala, and he *STILL* didn't notice it was a forgery!

It was *NOT* an exact copy! You didn't notice my **signature.**

Why would — What do you mean, *YOUR* signature?

I'm an **ALLIGATOR,** not a **FROG!**

She said "fraud".

Oh. It's hard to hear in these glasses.

Savanna, you may think people don't appreciate art as much as you. But if that were *true*, some artist, I don't know his name, wouldn't have *drawn* this **book** we're in.

Burp

And someone *ELSE* wouldn't be reading it right now.

Hi!

We're...in a **book?** I'm...just a **drawing?!**

Yes, we've recovered the art and caught the culprit. But though Savanna has committed crimes, she's certainly not EVIL. Copying the art isn't where she went wrong. It was her **belief** that there is only *one definition* of art, *one criteria* to judge an artist by and only *one way* to **appreciate** art.

Hopefully with some help, Savanna can come to realize she was **mistaken.**

Speaking of which, we need to be *takin'* these paintings to the museum again.

For the FIRST time, technically.

Whaddya say... skip ahead?

Skip ahead.

But **NO COW DETOURS!**

Chapter 18

The **COPYCAT** is in the bag! And by *BAG* I mean *JAIL*. This **cheetah** turned out to be a **CHEATER** who tried to replace historical masterpieces with her own imitations.

Art New-FAUX

For more, here's Vohnda Featherneck with the museum curator, Thelonious Snort.

It's **SNOOT**!

Yes, Cici. The priceless art is back and the museum's reputation is intact. In fact, all this excitement has generated a *renewed interest* in the art world.

Indeed!

The exhibit will be extended and opened to the public **free of charge,** since *NO ONE* got to see the actual paintings anyway. And thanks to **Councilman Fluffles,** the city has *fully funded* the museum's budget...

...in exchange for the museum dedicating a wing to **serious balloon art!**

All the museum's expenses will be paid. Including the **hospital bills** for everyone who got food poisoning!

VOTE

Well, let's hope everyone runs *TO* the museum and doesn't *GET* the runs *AT* the museum. Back to you, Cici!

Thanks for painting *THAT* picture for me, Vohnda.

Now, the weather.

Epilogue

Later...

&3 ART MUSEUM &3

I SURVIVED THE GALA

Now THAT'S art!

General Inspector! Isn't it impressive to see my *REAL* painting on display in the museum, surrounded by all this culture?

Hmm. *I feel bad saying this, Mango...* but I think I prefer the forgery!

WHAT?! But it's just a *COPY* of mine!

Beauty is in the EYE of the beholder, Mango.

And I'll *be holdin'* on to the one hanging in my office!

Wait, *YOU'RE* the artist who painted that? So was Macaroni Ancheese an **imposter?**

An im**PASTA!**

I was UNDERCOVER to catch the art thief. I'm an **AGENT of S.U.I.T.!**

Wow! Now *THAT'S* what I call *performance art!*

It's just like the end of **COLE'S LAW: THE MOVIE**, when Detective Cole joins **Agents** of S.A.L.A.D.: Super Awesome Lettuce And Disguises.

THAT'S IT!

IF YOU NEED ME, I'LL BE AT THE *MOVIES!*

THE END!

INVESTIGATORS

How to draw the COPYCAT

And remember: Copying is how many artists first learn how to draw!

1. Start with an upside-down egg shape, with the narrower part by her chin. Leave plenty of room on the page below for her body.

2. Draw half-circles on each side for ears and a triangle for her nose.

3. Draw a shape similar to a bowling pin or a soda bottle for her body.

4. Add arms and legs, plus hands and feet. Erase any unneccesary lines.

5. Draw facial features like eyes and a mouth, and her jacket and blouse.

6. Give her fingers and toes, and clothing details. Don't forget her tail!

7. This cheetah's not complete without her spots! Add some colour to make your drawings really come alive.

I'm... free?

8. Lastly, *ERASE HER BEFORE SHE ESCAPES!*

Gimme that!

I'm gonna draw my way outta this book!

Mango and **Brash** will return in their next book, *All Tide Up!*

For the latest in Gator news, activities, and more, visit **InvestiGatorsBooks.com**